In memory of my grandmother,
Beatrice Evelyn Harvey (nee Bairstow)
1883–1972

Little Hare Books
an imprint of
Hardie Grant Egmont
Ground Floor, Building 1, 658 Church Street
Richmond, Victoria 3121, Australia

www.littleharebooks.com

Copyright © Jan Ormerod 2004

First published 2004
First published in paperback 2005
This edition published 2013

Cataloguing-in-Publication details are available from the National Library of Australia

978-1-742976-78-5 (pbk.)

Designed by Kerry Klinner
Cover design by Hannah Robinson, Xou Creative
Produced by Pica Digital, Singapore
Printed through Asia Pacific Offset
Printed in Shenzhen, Guangdong Province, China

5 4 3 2 1

LIZZIE NONSENSE

Jan Ormerod

LITTLE HARE
www.littleharebooks.com

When Lizzie's mama and papa were married, the sun shone on fields of yellow wheat which grew right up to the door of the tiny church. But for as long as Lizzie can remember, she and Mama and Papa and baby have lived in their little house in the bush, and the church and neighbours are far away.

When Papa takes the sandalwood
he has cut into town, it is fifty miles
along sand tracks, and he will
be away a long time.

Then Lizzie and Mama and baby are all alone
in the little house in the bush.

Lizzie is always playing and pretending.
She is always dreaming.

'Lizzie nonsense!' her mama calls it.

Every morning, Lizzie and Mama carry water from the
creek for the vegetable patch and baby's bath.

Lizzie blows bubbles to make baby laugh.
'You're afloat in a boat on a big, wide sea,' she sings.
'You and your nonsense!' says her mama.

Then Lizzie picks flowers while Mama tends the garden.

'I'm a bride,' says Lizzie. 'Look at my beautiful bouquet.'
'What a lot of nonsense!' says her mama. 'Brides carry roses.'

There is always work to be done inside the house, too.

While Mama scrubs the table, Lizzie says,
'This house is as pretty as a picture.'
'Lizzie,' says her mama, 'you are full of nonsense.'

Sometimes a snake might crawl in and sleep under the rug,
and Lizzie and baby must sit on the table until
Mama has chased it out.

'You're the bravest mama in the world!' says Lizzie.
'Nonsense!' says Mama.

In the evening, Lizzie helps Mama prepare dinner.

'Tonight,' says Lizzie, 'we will eat peaches,
and cream, and little sweet cakes.'
'Such nonsense!' says her mama. 'We are
having turnips as usual.'

After dinner, when baby is asleep, there is usually
some mending to be done.

'I am making a party dress with lots of frills
and lace and bows,' says Lizzie.
'What an imagination,' says her mama.

But Lizzie's mama likes to imagine, too.
Every Sunday they put on their best clothes
and put baby in his pram.
Then they walk along the track and back,
and Mama pretends they have been to church.

Lizzie and her mama wish that the dingoes
howling outside at night were just imagination.

'I'm going to sleep in your bed to keep you safe,'
says Lizzie.

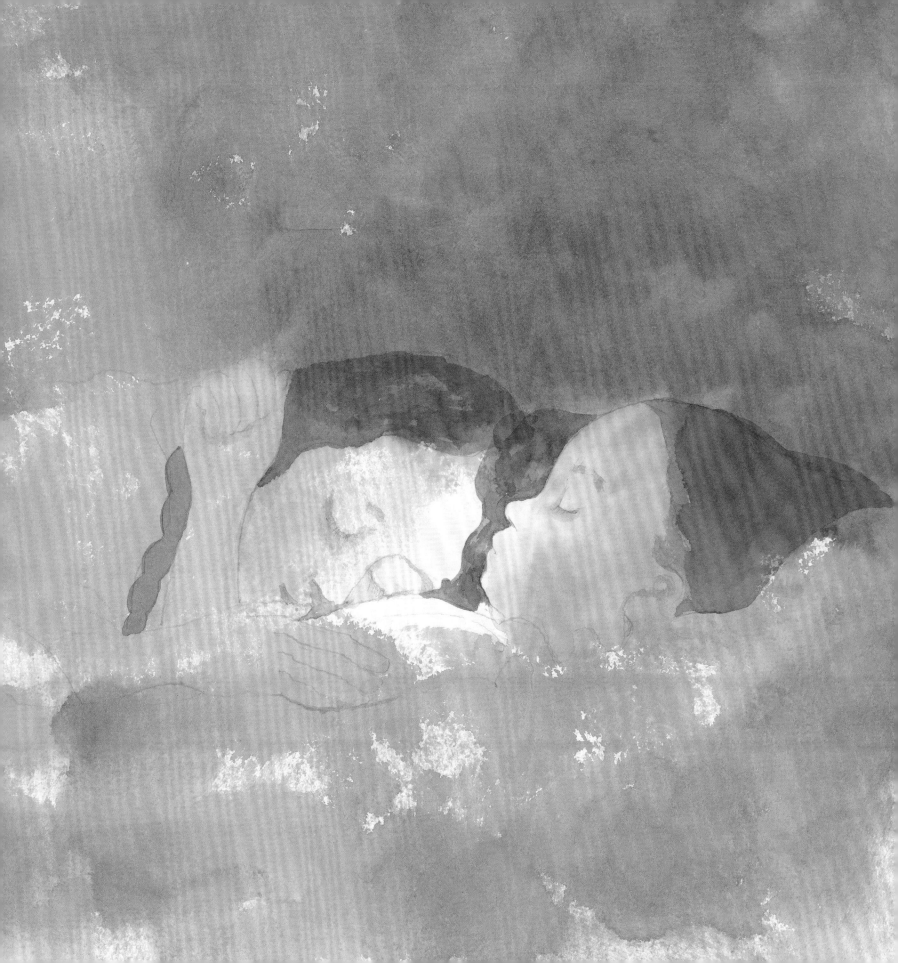

Finally one morning, after many weeks have passed,
Lizzie cries: 'What can I see? Is that a dust cloud
from my papa's team of horses?'
'Nonsense!' says her mama. 'It's your
head that is in the clouds.'

'But is my imagination playing tricks on me?'
wonders Mama. 'For I can hear harnesses jangling and
the dog barking. Make haste, Lizzie, make haste!'

They pick up baby and run helter-skelter down the track
towards Papa and the horses.

Papa lifts Lizzie high into the air and sits her on Bessie's
broad back. Then he takes Mama in his arms.
'You are as pretty as a picture, Beatrice,' he says.
'Pretty as the day we were married,
you with your white dress and bouquet of yellow roses.'

'Nonsense, Albert!' says Mama.
'And you,' he says to Lizzie,
'are as brave and pretty as your mother.'
'Nonsense!' says Lizzie.

And they walk together back to their
little house in the bush.